DEDICATED TO:

JACKSON KYLE ROLOFF

(MY FIRST GRANDSON)

© 2017 by Matt Roloff

Published by Matt Roloff Media

23985 NW Grossen Drive, Hillsboro, OR 97124

www.MattRoloffMedia.com

 RealMattRoloff

ISBN: 978-0-692-90660-6

Library of Congress Control Number: 2017909670

Printed in the United States of America

18 19 20 21 22 23 24 (BM) 10 9 8 7 6 5 4 3 2

Little Lucy
BIG
RACE

MATT ROLOFF

ILLUSTRATED BY:
RICK MARCKS

EDITED BY: Lauren Lodder
CONTRIBUTOR: Danielle Gonzales

MATT ROLOFF MEDIA

Pitter, Patter, Mitter, Matter.
On a beautiful day in the month of May
four fluffy puppies were born—

inside a barn, on Roloff Farms
atop a bale of hay.

Teeny, Tiny, Meeny, Miny.
Lucy was the smallest dog,
the underdog of her litter.

She'd sit sadly on the sidelines
and wish she were a bit bigger.

She was often stepped on *(Ow!)* by the big animals on the farm.

"**Baa**-ck up!" said lamb.
"**Moo**-ve over!" urged cow.
Goat added, "We **Mee**-an you no harm!"

Tritter, Trotter, Sitter, Sadder.
Lucy dreamed of playing too,
of making friends the way dogs do.

But little Lucy, much too shy,
could only sit alone and sigh.

"Say!" said Sully, passing by.
"I'll be your friend. Do not cry!"

You must have faith that you can do anything you put your heart into.

Dish, Dash, Flish, Flash.
Though little Lucy was small,
Wowee! Could she run fast!

None of the other farm animals
could keep up as she zoomed past.

The next day while Lucy was out playing, she stopped and happened to see a sign that read,

—JOIN THE—

BIG DOG RACE

HAVE SOME FUN!
RUN ALONG!
BE ALL YOU CAN BE!

Griff, Gruff, Riff, Ruff.
Lucy thought, *Could it be?*

Boy oh boy, a race for me?
I may be small, but they will see,
just how fast Lucy can be.

Off she raced to talk to Sully,
her new buddy, her big dog friend.

Sully told her, "You've got the talent,
but you must train until the end."

Splish, Splash, Mish, Mash.
Lucy practiced all day long,
in the sunshine, in the rain,

her muscles growing bigger, stronger,
as she ran and RAN again.

Into the mud, Lucy starts to slip.
Her foot gives way; she takes a dip.

I'm sad I fell, she stops and thinks,
but even big dogs sometimes trip.

Piddle, Paddle, Middle, Maddle.
She shakes her paws off, one by one,
checks for owies, just in case,

gets back up and starts to run,
a smile spread across her face.

At last, AT LAST the race is here.
Lucy knows the end is near.

Her heartbeat starts a steady climb,
as she spots the starting line. *(Oh, dear!)*

Huff, Puff, Struggle, Wuggle.
She slips her racing jersey on;
it's far too big, too loose, too long.

Dogs left and right are standing tall.
They look so fast, so fit, so strong.

Then ready, set, here we go!
The bell rings *(briiing!)* but no, no, NO.

Lucy falls behind the show.
She's running steady but slow, slow, SLOW.

Slow Go, Heave Ho.
Suddenly… something changes—

her jersey flips, becomes a cape.
Her little body re-arranges.
Her paws become a different shape.

The crowd begins to cheer and clap.
She only has just one more lap.

As Little Lucy picks up speed,
somehow, she takes the lead!

Wiggle, Waggle, Yay, Hooray!
Yes, Lucy did it! And just in time.
She's the first to cross the finish line.

Proving to herself
and everyone that day...

We are ALL special
in our own *little* way.

(Hooray!)

MATT ROLOFF

Photo by Michael Peterson

is one of a kind! He is an entrepreneur, farmer, actor, motivational speaker, author and star of the hit TLC reality docu-series "Little People Big World," which takes place on his farm in Oregon.

For over 13 years, Matt and his family have entertained millions of viewers and have earned a special place in the hearts of fans all over the world.

Matt was born with diastrophic dysplasia, a type of dwarfism, and walks with the use of crutches. He and Amy have four grown children, all of average height, except Zachary. Despite their differences, the Roloff family continues to thrive and overcome adversity. They have proven they can do everything a "typical family" can do, but just in a different way.

It's Matt's personal story that has inspired so many. Social stigmas and physical limitations are seen by Matt as opportunities NOT obstacles. Matt is a big thinker and an even bigger dreamer who thrives when faced with challenges. Matt is constantly crafting ways to move forward in reaching his goal of living an EXTRAORDINARY life.

Matt's inspiring nature and motivating spirit are evident in this unique and inspiring book. In *Little Lucy Big Race*, Matt demonstrates that we all have potential and are special in our own way.